THE MONTH BY MONTH A YEAR GOES ROUND

by Carol Diggory Shields
illustrated by True Kelley

DUTTON CHILDREN'S BOOKS) NEW YORK

FOR ZOOEY, WITH LOVE—C.D.S.

FOR MY NIECE ELOISE—T.K.

Text copyright © 1998 by Carol Diggory Shields
Illustrations copyright © 1998 by True Kelley

CIP Data is available.

Published in the United States 1998 by Dutton Children's Books.
a member of Penguin Putnam Inc.
375 Hudson Street. New York. New York 10014
Designed by Amy Berniker
Manufactured in China
First Edition
ISBN 0-525-45458-6
1 3 5 7 9 10 8 6 4 2

The sun comes up, the moon goes down,
By tick and tock a day goes round.
The days go dancing, one by one,
When seven pass, a week is done.
The moon is counting in the sky,
As week by week a month goes by.
Month by month the seasons swing,
Summer, autumn, winter, spring.
The moon comes up, the sun goes down,
And month by month a year goes round.

January, February, new blue boots,
Scarf and mittens, red snowsuit.

Scrunching, crunching,
making tracks,
Chilly tickles
down our backs.

Sweet hot cocoa in a thick white cup,
January, February, bundle up.

March and April,
drip-drop-drip,

Everything is melting
with a plip-plop-plip.

Shining puddles all around
Show a world that's upside down.

May and June
all down our street,

The trees are pink
from head to feet,
Like bridesmaids waiting
side by side.

Here I am!
Here comes the bride!

Petals twirling
on the breeze,
May and June,
dance with the trees.

July and August,
sizzle and pop,

Hot dogs sputter
and hot feet hop.

Hydrant pours an icy stream.

Jump and spray
and duck and scream.

Ice cream melts
and sparklers fizzle,

July and August,
pop and sizzle.

September, October, orange and round,
School bus moving through the town.

Pumpkins piled up in the sun,
Help me pick the perfect one!

Dry leaves skitter on the ground,
September, October, orange and brown.

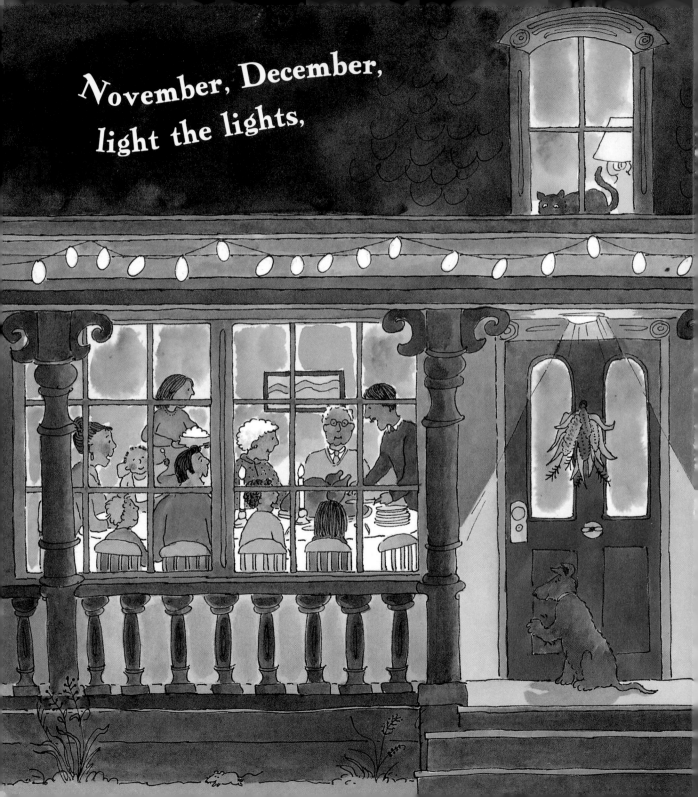

November, December,
light the lights,

Shining out through cold, dark nights.

Doorbells, hugs,
hellos, and kisses,

Aunts are laughing
over dishes.

Uncles tease and cousins grin,

November, December, come on in!

Now the year is at an end,
But January starts it up again.